A FLIP-FLOP ADVENTURE!

Flip-Flop
and the
Bully Frogs Gruff

By Janice Levy

Illustrated by
Colleen Madden

magic wagon

visit us at www.abdopublishing.com

Published by Magic Wagon, a division of the ABDO Group, 8000 West 78th Street,
Edina, Minnesota 55439. Copyright © 2012 by Abdo Consulting Group, Inc.
International copyrights reserved in all countries. All rights reserved. No part of this
book may be reproduced in any form without written permission from the publisher.

Looking Glass Library™ is a trademark and logo of Magic Wagon.

Printed in the United States of America, North Mankato, Minnesota.
052011
092011
 This book contains at least 10% recycled materials.

Written by Janice Levy
Illustrations by Colleen Madden
Edited by Stephanie Hedlund and Rochelle Baltzer
Cover and interior design by Jaime Martens

Library of Congress Cataloging-in-Publication Data

Levy, Janice.
  Flip-Flop and the Bully Frogs Gruff / by Janice Levy; illustrated by Colleen Madden.
    p. cm. – (A Flip-Flop adventure)
  Summary: Flip-Flop challenges each of the bullies who do not want to let her cross the bridge.
  ISBN 978-1-61641-653-9
  [1. Frogs–Fiction. 2. Animals–Fiction. 3. Bullies–Fiction.] I. Madden, Colleen M., ill II. Title.
  PZ7.L5832Flm 2011
  [E]–dc22
                        2010048712

Three Bully Frogs Gruff lived under a bridge.
If you tried to cross over, they got hopping mad.

They were gruff, tough, and buff.

One day, Flip-Flop strutted by.

"Hey, wart face!"
teased the first Bully Frog Gruff.
"What's with those blue suede shoes?"
He chinned himself on a branch.

"Move it or lose it!
I'm bad to the bone.
This bridge isn't big enough
for the two of us," he said.

Flip-Flop's knees bumpity bumped.

She wiped the sweat from her face.
Then she said, "I've places to go and friends to see.
Let's be **pals.** Don't **bully** me."

"RRRRibit!" bellowed the Bully Frog Gruff.
"I'll flatten you like a **bug-berry pancake**
and eat you for breakfast!"

"Not so fast," Flip-Flop warned.
"If you eat me, you'll get too **fat**."

"Fat? Not that!"
The Bully Frog sucked in
his belly and backed off.

"Hey, mud mouth!"
teased the second Bully Frog Gruff.
"I love your hair—NOT!"
She jogged in place.

"Move it or lose it!
I'm bad to the bone.
This bridge isn't big enough
for the two of us," she said.

Flip-Flop's knees **bumpity bumped.**
Her stomach **jumpity jumped.**

She wiped the sweat from her face.
Then she said, "I've places to go and friends to see.
Let's be **pals**. Don't **bully** me."

"RRRRibit!" bellowed the Bully Frog Gruff. "I'll roll you like a **worm burrito** and eat you for lunch!"

"Not so fast," Flip-Flop warned. "If you eat me, you'll grow a **double chin**."

"My chin? You win!" The bully frog covered her face and backed off.

"Hey, roach breath!"
teased the third Bully Frog Gruff.
"My goodness, sequins in July?"
He pumped rocks over his head.

Flip-Flop's knees bumpity bumped.
Her stomach jumpity jumped.
Her heart thumpity thumped.

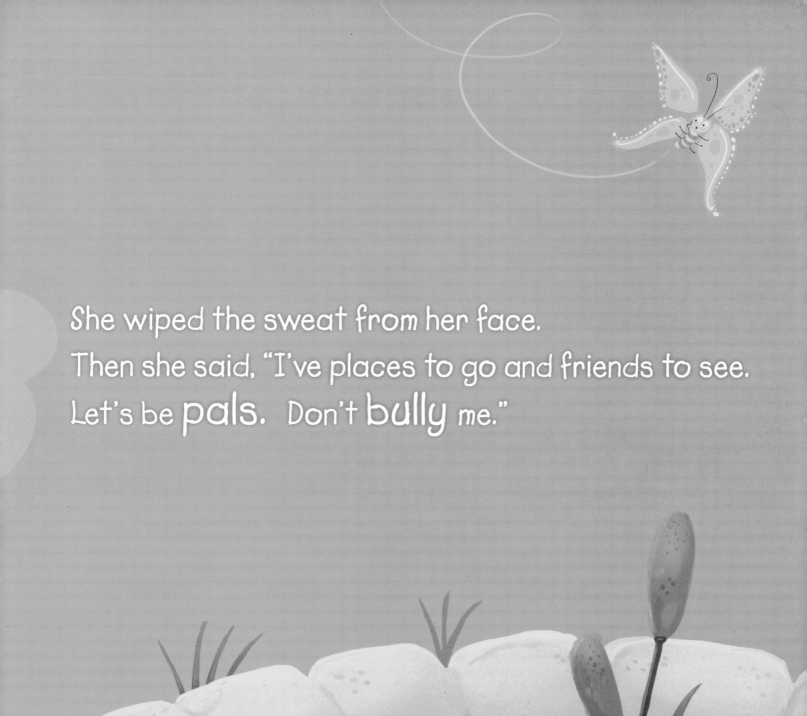

She wiped the sweat from her face.
Then she said, "I've places to go and friends to see.
Let's be pals. Don't bully me."

"RRRRibit!" bellowed the Bully Frog Gruff.
"I'll crunch you like a **cricket casserole**
and eat you for dinner."

"Not so fast," warned Flip-Flop.
"If you eat me, you'll get saggy and baggy."

"Not buff? Enough!"
The bully frog kicked
his legs and backed off.
He hid with the others.

"Yessss!" Flip-Flop tweeted.

"Hop on over. **Party** on the bridge!"

They sang karaoke and danced the afternoon away.

"See, this bridge is big enough for all of us," said Flip-Flop.

The **Bully Frogs** agreed.

So they cooked up some healthy party snacks and joined their new **friends.**

Flip-Flop FUN

Have you ever been bullied? What did you do? Here are some tips from Flip-Flop for dealing with bullies:

1. Stand up for yourself. Stay calm and confident and tell that bully that you don't like being talked to that way.

2. Try turning a mean rumor or comment into a joke.

3. Hold your head high, look your bully in the eye, and don't let him or her take away your self-esteem!

4. Try just listening to what they say. Let them know their words aren't going to get to you. It is no fun for them to bully someone who doesn't fight back or get scared.

About the Author: Janice Levy is the author of numerous award-winning children's books. Topics include bullying, multiculturalism, foster care, intergenerational relationships, and family values. She teaches creative writing at Hofstra University. Her adult fiction is widely published in magazines and anthologies.

About the Illustrator: Colleen Madden is an illustrator, mom, kickboxer, ukulele strummer, and honorary frog. She loves to draw for kids (and kids at heart!) and make people giggle. Flip-Flop is her third series of children's books. She is currently writing her own titles as author/illustrator, which will all be very silly books.